Hallow

Hi-Jinx

A Holiday Pet Sleuth

Mystery

ANNEE JONES

Halloween Hi-Jinx
Copyright©2022 Anne Kemerer Jones
All Rights Reserved

Cover Designer: V. McKevitt

Editor/Proofreader/ Formatter: Susan Horsnell

Table of Contents

Cast of Characters

Clarissa Bell (26)—Manager of Paws-N-Pastries

Velma Norwood (53)—Owner of Paws-N-Pastries

Harriet Twombly (45)—Cook

Darcy Shelton (19)—Server

Cody Shelton (28)—Darcy's older brother, Police Officer

Fletcher Conroy (20)—Server

Margo and Bubba Whitaker (mid-50s)—Jinx's previous owners

Landon Whitaker—Margo's and Bubba's son

Eddie Paige (48)—County Animal Shelter employee

Simone Laveau (27)—Owner, Envy women's clothing boutique

Alfred Squiggly (56)—Physics professor, New Haven College

Evan Lindstrom—Clarissa's ex-boyfriend

Jinx—Cat

Miss Louise—Cat

One-Eyed Willie—Cat

Twinkletoes and Sparklenose—Twin Kittens

Chapter One

Clarissa

A howl of wind rattled the windowpanes, sending the rainfall at a slant. It pounded against the thick glass like a drum roll. Clarissa watched through the large bay window at the front of the café as the tops of the tall elm and sycamore trees thrashed and bent in the autumn gale as though in an epic battle with Mother Nature. Thankful to be safe and indoors, she continued going over the day's receipts as closing hour approached.

"Is there anything else you'd like me to do before I leave?" asked Darcy Shelton, one of the two servers who worked part-time at the Paws-N-Pastries cat cafe. Clarissa smiled at the young college student as she finished wiping down the empty tables. Even though her appearance was a little shocking at first, underneath the dyed jet-black hair, rows of ear piercings, and dramatic eyeliner, Darcy shared the same tender heart for animals as she did.

"Nope," Clarissa said. "Harriet is still in the back, right?"

"Yes, she's just finishing in the kitchen. Did you try one of the chocolate-chip muffins she baked today? They were amazing."

Clarissa smiled and patted her slender stomach. "I'm glad they sold out before I ate them all by myself," she laughed. "I'm fine with closing up tonight. Velma said she might stop in to drop off additional supplies for the Black Cat Bash this weekend anyway."

"I'm so glad she hired you," said Darcy. "Velma's seemed really stressed lately. I know how much she wants the café's first charity event to be a success."

Clarissa nodded. "We all do," she replied. "The more money we can raise to help care for shelter cats, the better. Let's hope the investment we made in advertising the Halloween party in the neighboring counties brings in more people."

Especially since she'd had to convince Velma the expense would be worth it according to the numbers she ran. This was her chance to prove that she could handle a position in restaurant management, and she didn't want to think about what would happen if she failed. The mere thought of heading back home to Stamford with her tail between her legs made her shudder. This was the perfect opportunity to use the skills she'd put herself through college by waiting tables to learn. She'd always hoped to use her business degree to help animals in some way as well. Given that she was squeamish at the sight of blood, becoming a veterinarian or veterinary technician had never been feasible career paths.

Following graduation, she'd been hired as a call center representative for a credit card company. But after eight months of dealing with angry customers and scam artists, she was determined to find a job where she could actually do something to make a difference. When she saw the ad in the paper for the position of manager for the Paws-N-Pastries cat cafe in New Haven, billed as "a halfway house" for homeless cats, she jumped at the opportunity even though it would mean she'd have to move to the small town an hour away. She'd thought it was a dream come true when Velma hired her immediately following a telephone interview.

Darcy disappeared into the back and returned a few minutes later with her coat and purse. She was shrugging into her jacket when the cafe phone rang.

"I'll get it," said Clarissa, rising from the table where she was sitting with the paperwork. She walked around the counter and grabbed the receiver.

"Good evening, Paws-N-Pastries. This is Clarissa speaking."

"Hey Clarissa, it's Eddie down at the county shelter. You got a sec?"

"Sure, what's up?"

"You know how maxed out we are down here, and I have a husband and wife who just walked in wanting to turn over their cat. Do you have room at the café to take another one?"

"Sure," Clarissa said. "We just placed Daisy and Tulip with a wonderful family this past week, so we have space."

"Fantastic," Eddie said with a sigh. "Can't tell you how glad we are that Velma finally got the license to house cats at the café there in New Haven. We're receiving more adoptable animals than we've been able to place with our limited government resources."

"I know," Clarissa said, all too aware of the problem. "We're hoping the Black Cat Halloween Bash this weekend will raise funds to help care for the homeless animals as well as spread the word about how important it is for people to have their pets spayed and neutered."

"Agreed," Eddie replied. "I'll let these folks know you can take their cat. They want to turn it over now. How late will you be open?"

Clarissa glanced at the clock. It was 8:30PM and the café normally closed at 9:00PM.

Her eyes slid to the only customer remaining, a disheveled physics professor from the local college who preferred to work out his equations over mochaccinos with three shots of mint flavoring and extra whipped cream. He sat hunched over his laptop at a corner table, where he'd been perched since just after noon. Empty coffee cups and a plate with a half-eaten turkey club littered the table's wooden surface along with a scattering of crumpled papers. She smiled ruefully. The professor, whose name she'd learned was Alfred Squiggly, stared at the numbers shining on his computer screen, completely unaware of the piece of dark-green spinach that had been lodged in his white beard all afternoon.

"I'll wait," she said, knowing the drive from the shelter in Stamford was about an hour.

"Thanks, you're a lifesaver," said Eddie.

"Are we getting a new kitty?" asked Darcy, fastening the buttons on her navy jacket.

Clarissa clicked off the call and placed the receiver into the cradle. "Yep, looks that way." She glanced into the area of the restaurant they referred to as the Kitty Corner, which was dedicated to the care of the cats. The two permanent residents of the café, a gray tabby named Miss Louise and a balding calico with one eye named One-Eyed Willie, both seniors, were curled up on opposite ends of an emerald-green couch, sound asleep. "You two are going to be getting a new friend soon," she called.

Willie lifted his head, blinked his one eye, and then closed it again. Miss Louise got up, turned in a circle, and then lay back down with her back facing Clarissa.

"Obviously they're thrilled," laughed Darcy. "I wish I could stay and meet the new arrival, but my brother is picking me up tonight. My car's still in the shop, unfortunately."

"No problem. Although I'm sorry to hear about your car."

"Yeah, me too." Darcy pulled a face. "Apparently, they're still waiting for some part to come in that's going to cost me an arm and a leg. At least I don't have to spend money on a rental vehicle since my brother's offered to drive me back and forth to the café for my shifts. Luckily my apartment is close enough to the college so I can just walk."

At that moment, the bell over the front door jingled as it opened, revealing a man dressed in a dark-blue police uniform. His shiny silver badge caught the light reflecting off the crystals of the antique chandelier that hung in the foyer of the old red brick building.

Clarissa sucked in her breath. He was quite possibly the most attractive man she'd ever laid eyes on. She'd had the same boyfriend all through college, but both she and Evan finally agreed the relationship wasn't going anywhere and called it quits before graduation. Since then, she'd been too focused on working and finding a meaningful job to think about dating again. "Officer? Is there a problem?"

The man smiled and shook his head. His wavy hair was the color of dark chocolate and curled over his forehead.

"Hi Cody," said Darcy, slinging her shabby-chic hobo bag over her shoulder. "Clarissa, this is my older brother, Cody. As you can see, he's a police officer."

Clarissa blew out a breath and laughed. "Phew. Sorry, you scared me for a minute there."

"Well, it is almost Halloween." Cody acknowledged while making his way over to them with a grin. "And the weather outside seems to be getting in the spirit." He held out his hand for a shake. "You must be the new manager here."

"Yes, I'm Clarissa Bell." She placed her hand in his. "Nice to meet you."

"Darcy told me you're new in town," he continued.

"That's right," she answered. "I moved here a little over a month ago."

"Let me know if you need someone to show you around. New Haven's a great little community if I do say so myself. Darcy and I have lived here our whole lives."

"I'd appreciate that, thanks." Clarissa gazed into Cody's twinkling eyes.

"Come on, bro." Darcy took her brother's hand. "I've got to study for an exam tomorrow. You do want me to become a nurse, right?"

"Absolutely. I couldn't be prouder of you, sis. It was nice meeting you, Clarissa. Stay safe tonight, it's blustery out there."

"Thanks," Clarissa responded. "You too." The duo wound their way back through the eating area to the entrance. Clarissa felt a burst of cold air as the door opened and shut again and shivered. She returned to the table where she'd been sitting going over the paperwork. She sat back down and stared at her notes for a few minutes but was unable to get the image of the handsome police officer out of her mind. Finally, she decided to fix herself a cup of hot tea.

She was just pouring hot water over a bag of her favorite variety, lemon ginger, when the owner of the café appeared from the cook's kitchen in a flowing black floor-length skirt, long-sleeved shirt with an image of a cat's face covered in silver sequins, and a purple scarf. At least one element of Velma Norwood's daily ensemble was always in a shade of purple since she declared it to be her favorite color in the rainbow. Her hair, however, was a shade of red not found anywhere in nature. Even from behind the coffee bar, Clarissa could see dark circles beneath Velma's eyes. Her hair was lank and damp, as if she hadn't bothered to cover her head while out in the rain.

"Hi Velma, I have some good news," she said. "County called – we're getting another cat to foster. Its owners are on their way now to surrender him."

The tired woman smiled faintly. "That's wonderful," she said. "I'm so glad word about the café is finally starting to spread. Let's just hope I can keep the place open." She ran a hand through her mussed hair and sighed. "I really hope you're right, Clarissa – that the Black Cat Bash will raise enough money to put us into the black. Otherwise, I'm not sure we'll be able to keep fostering animals here next year." Tears filled her eyes.

"Oh, no," Clarissa said, hurrying out the counter to give the older woman a hug. Unfortunately, she couldn't think of anything to say to reassure her since she was equally as worried about the establishment's financial picture. After she'd taken a first look at the books, she'd realized right away that the eccentric owner had a big heart but not a head for business.

"Black Cat Bash?" Professor Squiggly suddenly called from across the room. He pushed his wire-rimmed glasses up his reddened nose. "Hi there, Velma."

"Oh, hi Professor," Velma responded. "Yes, we're hosting a Halloween costume party here at the café on Saturday night. We decided to call it the Black Cat Bash. Tickets are $10."

"Hm." The professor scratched behind his ear. "To be honest, I've never really been a cat person. Or a dog person either, for that matter. I started coming here just for the coffee and Wi-fi. I'm working out a quantum physics problem, you see, and believe I'm on the brink of discovering the correct calculations to describe the thirteenth dimension. I'm planning to submit my theory for publication soon and time is of the essence. Unfortunately, I get terrible internet service at home."

"I understand," said Velma, her expression one of dejection. "Of course, you have better things to do than dress up for Halloween."

"But you're more than welcome to use the café's Wi-fi as much as you like," interjected Clarissa hurriedly. Even if the old professor wasn't particularly fond of animals, his patronage at the café would still contribute to the cause.

Professor Squiggly held up his hand. "However, with all the time I've been spending here lately, I believe I'm beginning to develop a fondness for the felines. There's something about One-Eyed Willie that kind of reminds me of myself if I must tell the truth. He seems to enjoy a good scratch about the ears, as I do myself," he said with a chuckle. "In short, I've come to look forward to seeing the creature when I come in. So maybe I'm turning out to be a cat person after all."

Clarissa smiled. Velma lifted one of the fringed ends of her purple scarf and dabbed her eyes.

"That makes me so happy," she said, turning to look at One-Eyed Willie who emitted a soft snore and back to the professor. "Would you like to buy a ticket to the Halloween party then?"

"Yes, I believe I shall," said Professor Squiggly, reaching for his wallet. "Do you have change for a $20?"

"Certainly," said Velma, going to the cash register. "Oh, Clarissa," she called as she rang up the sale. "Don't let me forget to lock the registers on Saturday before we start letting people in. With all the hullabaloo, I'm afraid I'll forget."

"No problem," said Clarissa, making herself a mental note.

Professor Squiggly accepted the little orange ticket from Velma and tucked it into his billfold with a smile. "I think I'll head on home now," he said, stifling a yawn. "If I don't stop in before the party, I'll see you all there."

"See you soon," said Velma. She turned to Clarissa as the older man powered off his laptop and began packing his belongings into a worn leather briefcase.

"I dropped off more supplies for the party in the storage room," she said. "Harriet wanted to make up the batter for a new cupcake recipe before she left for the evening. I'll go see how she's coming along."

"Sounds good," Clarissa said. "Darcy cleaned the cats' cages earlier this afternoon and I've already refreshed their bowls with clean water and kibble, so they'll be all set for the night. I'll wait here to greet the couple coming to surrender their cat and complete the necessary forms with them."

"Thank you, dear," said Velma, patting her on the shoulder and turning for the kitchen.

Retrieving her mug of tea, Clarissa opened a drawer for a clean teaspoon and scooped the teabag into the compost bin. She added cream and sugar to the steaming liquid and stirred languidly. The rain continued to fall steadily outside, and she listened to its pitter patter, sipping the warm beverage and patiently waiting for the café's last visitors.

Professor Squiggly retrieved his trench coat from the coat tree in the foyer and looped his arms into it. Reaching for the handle of his umbrella in the nearby canister, Clarissa was surprised when he popped it open. Wasn't opening an umbrella indoors considered bad luck?

With a wave goodbye, he opened the door and maneuvered himself and the open umbrella outside as a very stern-looking couple made their way inside with a pet carrier.

"This cat is cursed," the pale-faced woman carrying the box declared.

Chapter Two

Jinx

Inside the cat carrier, Jinx rolled his eyes. Oh, please. He was no more cursed than the girl with the curly blonde hair with the surprised look on her face he could see through the bars of his portable cage. He debated whether to hiss but figured it probably wouldn't make the best impression. He'd decide later if his new situation warranted a show of displeasure. Which it very well might. He poked his nose through the bars and sniffed. Hm. That was still to be determined.

The blonde lady swallowed. She set her mug down on the counter and hurried around to greet them.

"I'm Clarissa, the manager here," she said, accepting the carrier into her arms. He could smell traces of salmon on her sweater – if he wasn't mistaken, it was his favorite brand of kitty pate. Clarissa might a friend after all. His whiskers twitched with newfound hope.

"Cursed?" She continued. "What do you mean?"

"My name is Margo Whitaker," said his previous owner. "And this is my husband, Bubba."

"It's nice to meet you," replied Clarissa.

"Didn't the man from the shelter tell you why we wanted to turn him in when he phoned over here?" asked Bubba. Through the carrier, Jinx could see Bubba's bushy eyebrows knitting together as he shifted from foot to foot. Water dripped off the man's dirty work boots, leaving streaks of brown residue on the shiny floor.

"No." Clarissa shook her head, making her yellow curls bounce. "Eddie just said they were full downtown and asked if we could accept this little guy."

"Oh," said Bubba, hooking his right thumb underneath the suspender of his overalls nervously. "Well, you'll still take him off our hands, right?"

Please, let it be so, Jinx prayed, folding his paws one over the other. He didn't think he could stand another minute being trapped in the same house with these two.

"We definitely can't keep him," Margo said, taking a step backward and eyeing him as though he were one of the evils hiding within

Pandora's box. He blinked back at her innocently.

"You don't have to worry," Clarissa replied reassuringly. "You have my word that we'll take wonderful care of your cat while he's with us, and make sure he's placed into a loving forever family as well."

"Excellent," Margo said, exhaling in relief. "But please don't call him our cat, he was only with us for a short time and caused more trouble than all five of our children ever did, and they're all grown and out of the house."

That's it. The time had come. He wouldn't take the blame laying down any more. He had to stand up for himself and all of black cat-kind in the face of false accusations. Baring his teeth, he mustered his energy and uttered a low hiss.

Clarissa's forehead furrowed.

"Won't you come with me into the Kitty Corner—that's what we call the area set up to house and socialize the cats – and we can sit down and complete the necessary paperwork?"

"Of course," Margo said, straightening her spine. Her lips whitened as she stretched them into a polite smile. She clutched her purse tighter to her side.

The short ride in the carrier in Clarissa's arms was thankfully smooth—no excess jostling or tipping, which he very much appreciated. The day had been long enough, and he was ready for a nap and if all went as well as he hoped, a tasty treat before bedtime. Clarissa set the carrier down on an ottoman which he was glad to find offered him a panoramic view of the space.

There was an overstuffed green couch—with two cats at either end who were obviously pretending to be asleep when they were following what was happening more closely than a teenager on social media - and several chairs and tables set up in small groupings. Plush pillows and soft-looking throws in warm tones decorated the furniture. A thick Oriental rug overlaid the floor. A bank of open cat condos lined the far wall, each one containing bowls full of kibble and water, as well as a fur-lined bed and clean litter box. Jinx's mouth dropped open in wonder as he continued to survey the surroundings. Colorful feathers, scratching posts, and all sorts of toys were scattered around the room. A wide window perch sat underneath a picture window on the exposed-brick wall at the front, and if he wasn't mistaken, the series of shelves that ran above a tall cat tree served as a kitty climbing gym. Could this be heaven?

The calico on the left end of the sofa raised his head (Jinx could see he was missing some fur on top and there were a few grey whiskers sticking out of his ears)—and blinked his one yellow eye. "Nope, ain't heaven, but it sure is close, sonny boy," he said. "Welcome aboard. I'm known as One-Eyed Willie around these parts."

Jinx hadn't realized he'd spoken aloud in cat language.

"Hi," he replied to One-Eyed Willie. "This place looks amazing."

The tabby on the opposite side of the couch got up and settled onto her delicate haunches. She lifted her tiny, pointed nose in the air and stared at him haughtily as she licked her right foremost paw and slowly smoothed the fur over her shoulder into place. Not that it had been out of place before. Jinx had never seen such an immaculate cat.

"Good evening, child," said the prim tabby. "I am Miss Louise."

"Um, hello, ma'am," he replied.

One-Eyed Willie guffawed and jerked his fifth digit in Miss Louise's direction.

"She thinks she's in charge. Which she actually is, mind you."

Miss Louise fluttered her eyelashes. "Aw, you old coot."

Clarissa glanced around at the cats with a raised eyebrow and sat down in the chair nearest Jinx. Bubba planted himself with a loud exhale onto the sofa in the middle of One-Eyed Willie and Miss Louise, without appearing to have noticed the presence of either one. Both cats immediately jumped off and disappeared. Margo perched on the edge of a wingback chair, her purse in her lap.

"We found the cat one day—about three months ago or thereabouts. Isn't that right, hon?" began Bubba.

Margo nodded. "Yes, it was late last Spring," she said. "I remember because I had some come back from my Saturday quilting circle. Nina Edwards was hosting that day. Anyway, I came home about 4:00PM and went to water the hanging plants on the back porch before starting on supper. Right as I was watering the Devil's Ivy, I saw something black move underneath one of the boxwoods along the fence. I admit, I was curious, so I went to investigate."

"You know what they say about curiosity," Bubba remarked, shaking his head sadly.

Jinx was pleased to see Margo give him the side-eye.

"Anyhoo," she continued, "I discovered a little black cat. I assumed it was a kitten. It leaped into my arms and snuggled right in like I was his long-lost mother. So, I brought him inside the house and showed him to Bubba when he got home from work."

"And we named him Jinx, because he's all-black," continued Bubba. "We thought it was just a little joke, you know, because of the superstition about black cats being trouble at all."

Clarissa grimaced. "Unfortunately, that superstition has given black cats a bad name," she said.

"Unfortunately, in this case it seems to be true," said Margo seriously.

Jinx shook his head. She'd been doing so well.

"Right after we adopted him, all sorts of terrible things started happening," Bubba said, lowering his voice to a whisper.

Clarissa leaned forward. "Like what?"

"First, the dishwasher stopped working," said Margo, counting on her fingers. "Then, the basement flooded. And then, I baked a cake for the church fundraiser, and it fell flat! That hasn't happened to one of my cakes in 47 years." She pressed her lips together solemnly.

"And I got a rash!" said Bubba. "Want to see?" He bent down and began to unlace his boot.

"No, thank you," Clarissa said hurriedly. Jinx breathed a sigh of relief.

Clarissa stood and walked to a small desk in the far corner. She opened one of the drawers and removed a clipboard containing a sheaf of forms and a ballpoint pen. She brought them over to the Whitakers.

"If you'll both just sign, here," she said, handing the tablet and pen to Margo first.

After each of them had signed, Clarissa stepped in front of the cat carrier.

"Thank you," she said. "I'm sure you're both tired from your journey. Please don't let me keep you from a good night's rest."

"Yes, yes, quite right," said Margo, rising. "Come, Bubba."

"Yes, dear," he said, heaving himself off the couch with a huff. "After you."

Clarissa walked them swiftly to the entrance and showed them out.

"Safe travels," she called with a wave and then closed and locked the front door behind them,

Hurrying back to the Kitty Corner, she knelt and unfastened the locks on the carrier.

"Here you go, sweetie," she said. "I'm sorry that took so long."

Jinx leaped out. "I'm free!" he yelled with a whoop.

A loud crash sounded from the kitchen. Uh-oh.

Chapter Three

Clarissa

"I don't believe it," Clarissa whispered down to Jinx from the top of the stepstool. She was stringing fake spiderwebs in the corners of the café. Pleased with the wispy effect of the intersecting white strands, she popped a fake plastic spider in the middle and climbed back down. Jinx was busy scratching his claws on a nearby sisal scratching post. Given his small size, she would almost have mistaken him for a kitten. However, the Whitakers told her that their vet confirmed he was actually a full-grown adult cat, probably around the age of four or five. "There's no such thing as a cursed cat," she continued, talking as though Jinx could understand her. "Harriet dropping the glass bowl in the kitchen last night after you arrived was just a coincidence." Jinx looked up at her with big green eyes and yawned, revealing two neat rows of sharp white teeth.

"Aw, you are such a cutie," she said, bending down to give him a scratch under the chin. "I don't know how anyone could think you're the reason for their troubles." He purred in response. She giggled, recalling having run into the kitchen the night before to discover both the cook and Velma covered in flour from head-to-toe. Neither of them seemed to think the situation was as amusing as she did, though. After helping clean up, they'd all declared it a night. Clarissa had put the cats into their condos and closed the doors before she left, to allow Jinx a bit of privacy to rest. Of course, she'd made sure he had a full bowl of food in case the Whitakers hadn't given him dinner and dropped in several tuna-flavored treats, which he'd promptly gobbled up.

This morning, she was happy to find that his food bowl was empty. After refilling the food and water bowls for all three cats, she watched to see how they would get along with each other once they were allowed to roam freely. One-Eyed Willie and Miss Louise were their usual selves—neither minded the presence of other cats or people which made them the perfect permanent residents for Paws-N-Pastries. And, despite a few hisses from Jinx the previous evening, she hadn't heard him hiss once all morning.

She glanced towards Miss Louise, who was now preening in her cushioned cat bed after having eaten her breakfast. One-Eyed Willie sat in the lap of a small child, who was patting him on the head rather forcefully. She smiled. Willie always looked rather grumpy. Not only was the poor guy missing an eye, but most of teeth as well. As a result, his mouth curved down at the corners, which only added to his crotchety-seeming appearance. However, she knew he was just a big softie at heart. Sure enough, he held still and allowed the little girl to have her fun.

"Abby," called a woman dressed in yoga pants and a sweatshirt from the counter where she was picking up a to-go coffee and bag of snacks. "Remember to pet the kitty gently, like this." She demonstrated a long, gentle stroke.

"Yes, Mommy," the girl replied.

Clarissa was glad to see the child make an effort to copy her mother's gentle movement as she stroked Willie's fur more softly.

"Aren't these cute?" Velma asked, giggling as she pulled a handful of small, Halloween-inspired stuffed animals from an open cardboard box nearby. She held up a smiling ghost, bat, and pumpkin.

"They're adorable," laughed Clarissa.

"I found them at the thrift shop and couldn't resist," said Velma. "And look at this one." She pulled a larger cloth figure of a witch from the box. It looked like it had been hand-sewn, with a pointy black hat and cape made from pieces of felt, green-and-white striped stockings, and black shoes that curled up at the toes. Strands of green yarn served for hair. A tiny black cat sat on one of the witch's shoulders, and it clasped a broomstick made from wrapped-together twigs in one of its hands.

"That's fantastic," agreed Darcy. "Why don't you prop the Wicked Witch up in front of the register?"

"Great idea," said Velma, walking over to position it so it sat on the ledge of the counter and leaned against the register's back with its legs hanging down off the edge.

"That looks great," called Clarissa from the Kitty Corner. She picked up the stool and moved it against the far wall of the eating area. She thought maybe she'd tape up some of the cute friendly ghost cut-outs she'd discovered within the assortment of party supplies.

"Oh, by the way," said Darcy as she pushed the register drawer closed. "Cody should be stopping by to deliver the pumpkins any minute."

"Cody's delivering pumpkins?" Clarissa repeated. She didn't think she'd see him again so soon and felt her pulse pick up speed.

"Yep," said Darcy. "The wife of one of the guys down at the station comes from a family that owns a vegetable farm not too far away. Apparently, their pumpkin patch has a surplus of gourds this year, so Cody offered to bring over some of the extras to help us decorate for the Black Cat Bash tomorrow night."

"Fantastic," said Velma, clapping her hands together. "There's no such thing as too many decorations, after all."

"I agree," said Darcy, fingering the row of silver piercings in her ear.

Clarissa shook her head and smiled. She loved decorating and dressing up for the holidays as much as anyone, but unlike the other women who both enjoyed wearing rather dramatic makeup and loud colors on an everyday basis, she preferred minimal makeup and simple clothing in neutral shades most days of the year.

"Hey, everyone," called a male voice. A young, thin man in his early twenties with a brown ponytail appeared from the back. He was dressed in jeans, a flannel shirt, and hiking boots.

"Hi, Fletcher," said Velma. "Coming in for your shift?"

"Yep, I'm on in an hour, so I figured I'm come in early and help out with party preparations. Kind of beats studying for my abnormal psych final next week," he said with a laugh.

Darcy had told Clarissa that Fletcher Conroy, the café's other part-time server, attended New Haven College as well. He was studying to become a mental health counselor.

"So, where's this cursed cat I've been hearing about?" Fletcher asked, joining them amid the bags and boxes of party supplies.

"Cursed cat?" asked Velma, her hand flying to her chest. "What do you mean?"

Fletcher shrugged. "Landon Whitaker is in one of my classes. He knows I work here and told me that his parents were going to bring their cat here to put it up for adoption because they'd got this crazy idea that it's cursed."

"Clarissa?" Velma asked, turning to her with widened eyes. "Do you know anything about this?"

"Oh, surely you don't believe a silly superstition," said Clarissa, coming over to gather the paper ghosts and tape. "Jinx is harmless."

Velma looked over at the cat, who had hopped up on the back of the couch and sat there, watching them. Velma twisted the ends of her purple scarf worriedly. "I sure hope you're right," she said. Clarissa was close enough to hear her mutter more softly, "Because I really don't need any more trouble right now than I already have."

Clarissa knew she was worried about the café's finances, but even if the Halloween party didn't bring in as much money as they hoped, it didn't mean they couldn't put their heads together to come up with more ways to raise money to help the homeless animal problem in the county.

She was halfway through hanging the row of smiling ghosts when the bell over the front door jingled.

"Hi Cody," called Darcy from the coffee bar.

"Hi Sis," he said. "Hey there, Clarissa."

She paused and twisted around on the stepladder. At that moment, Jinx scampered underneath and the suddenness of the movement caught her off guard. Her foot slipped on the rung and she fell backward, landing on the hard tile with a thud.

Cody dropped the box of pumpkins in the entry and rushed over to her.

"Are you okay?" he asked, kneeling. "Where does it hurt?"

Clarissa rubbed her elbow where it had made contact with the stone. She pushed up her sleeve and sure enough, the area was already turning black and blue. Her cheeks flamed with heat, and she wasn't sure which was worse – the throbbing in her elbow or the pain of embarrassment. "It's just a bruise," she said with a half-hearted laugh as she met Cody's concerned gaze.

"I'll get some ice," called Darcy.

"I'm so sorry," said Cody. "I didn't mean to startle you. Here, let me help you up."

He lifted her easily off the floor. He was close enough that she could smell the spicy scent of his aftershave and another rush of heat coursed through her body. He was dressed in plainclothes today, jeans and an open jacket over a simple blue shirt.

She shook her head. "It wasn't your fault. Or Jinx's," she said. "Just a clumsy moment, I'm afraid."

Velma groaned.

"What's wrong?" asked Cody, turning around.

"Oh, we got a new surrender last night," said Clarissa. "Come meet Jinx. Apparently, his previous owners have started a silly rumor that he's cursed, and trouble follows him just because of the color of his fur."

She led him over to the cat and picked him up. Jinx snuggled into her arms and started to purr.

"Aw, he's so cute," said Cody, holding out his fingers so Jinx could sniff and then petting him gently. "After our parents died, I got a cat for Darcy from the county shelter. Remember Marshmallow?" he said as his sister brought over a towel full of ice.

"I sure do," she said, touching the towel to Clarissa's elbow.

"Let me take that," said Cody, cocking his head to the counter. "You've got more customers lining up over there and I'm going to grab Fletcher here in a sec to help me bring in more pumpkins."

"Okay," said Darcy, passing him the towel.

"Thanks," said Clarissa as he held it to her elbow.

"Of course," Cody said with a smile. "Your hands are full at the moment, but it's important that we get ice on that bruise right away to keep the swelling down."

"I'm so sorry to hear about your parents," said Clarissa.

He nodded. "Yeah, me too. They were killed in a car accident when I was 20 and Darcy was just 11. Thankfully I'd already completed training and was hired as a new recruit on the New Haven PD so I had an income stream to be able to take care of my sister."

"Wow, you raised her on your own?" Clarissa was amazed.

He shrugged. "Honestly, adopting that cat was one of the best decisions I ever made. Marshmallow wasn't in good condition when we got him and caring for him not only helped him heal, but us, too."

Clarissa blinked back tears and she cuddled Jinx. "I can relate to that," she said quietly. "My parents divorced when I was three, and my dad basically left us. My mom worked all the time after that to make ends meet. Our cat, Lily, was the closest thing I had to a sibling growing up."

"Ah," said Cody. "I guess that explains our mutual love of pets."

She nodded. "Absolutely."

The bell over the door jingled again, and a woman with long, stick-straight dark hair wearing a tight leopard print dress and stiletto boots tottered in waving a fifty-dollar bill. She looked like she should be going to a photo shoot instead of walking into a small-town café. Clarissa wondered whether she was someone famous. Since she didn't watch much television, she wouldn't recognize a celebrity even if she met one face to face.

"Hello!" The woman called in a practiced sing-song voice. "Who works here?"

"I do," said Clarissa. "My name is Clarissa Bell, I'm the manager. Can I help you?"

The woman walked over, eyeing Cody with obvious appreciation. "My name is Simone Laveau," she said, fluttering her impossibly long eyelashes. "I just opened Envy next door – you know, the women's fashion boutique."

"Oh, you're the owner?" asked Velma, joining them. "I'm Velma Norwood. I opened Paws-N-Pastries earlier this year and have been watching the remodeling next door—that space used to be a chiropractor's office," she explained to Clarissa. "I've been meaning to stop by to do some shopping. The clothes in your displays look fabulous. I love what you're wearing now."

"Thank you," said Simone politely. She set her hands on her slender waist and spun in a circle. "This dress was created by one of my favorite designers. We carry it in several sizes." She stopped and looked at Velma up and down. "Although I'd have to check to see whether it's available in yours."

"Oh—of course," Velma murmured.

Simone smiled and waved her manicured hand. "I can always place a custom order though," she said. "For an additional charge as I'm sure you understand." She turned to Cody.

"And are you one of these ladies' husbands?" she asked pointedly.

He shook his head. "Afraid I don't have that honor," he said. "I'm Cody Shelton. The girl over at the counter is my little sister."

"Oh, I see," Simone said brightly. "Do you work here too, Cody?"

"No again," he said, chuckling. "I'm on the force here—member of New Haven police department."

Clarissa noticed Jinx narrowing his eyes in her arms. She wondered if the cat agreed with her that Simone's sights were clearly set on Cody.

"Um, did you need something?" she asked.

"Yes," Simone responded, sliding her gaze in her direction. "Could you run along and get me some change for this fifty? I have a customer waiting next door and figured it would faster to walk over here than make a trip to the bank."

"Sure," Clarissa replied, regretting she'd asked. She turned with Jinx still in her arms and headed for the cash register, angry at the green monster of jealousy who'd suddenly appeared in her heart.

Chapter Four

Jinx

"Willie!" Miss Louise flicked him on the top of his head with her tail from her perch on the cat tree, which was one level above where he sat gaping at Simone.

"Put your eye back in your head! You're a cat, not a human, remember?"

"Harrumph!" said Willie, twitching his whiskers. "Just because I'm not the same species doesn't mean I can't appreciate feminine beauty! Why, I'll bet that woman has a litter of 20 babies at home with all that milk she's carrying around!"

Miss Louise rolled her eyes. "Remind me to explain some things to you, my friend," she said.

Jinx wandered over to them from where Clarissa had set him down by the coffee bar. Hopping up to the couch, he stretched his back and had a seat.

"I didn't mean to make Clarissa fall, honest," he said. "It was an accident, cat's honor."

"Sure," said Willie.

"We know that honey," said Miss Louise. "Humans often place blame where it doesn't belong. We've got your back, sweetie. Your reputation is safe with us."

"Thanks," said Jinx, exhaling in relief. "By the way, I don't know about you guys, but I'm getting the sense that Simone's trying to get her hooks into Cody. Anyone with me?"

"Yeah, I got that too," said Willie, nodding. "Wonder if he'll take the bait? I'm not sure I really see them together, though."

"Agreed," said Miss Louise, lying down and crossing one front paw over the other daintily. "Frankly, so many of that woman's layers are fake I'm having difficulty getting much of a read on her."

"Yeah," said Jinx. "I was up close, and her perfume was so strong I was about to sneeze when Clarissa thankfully moved me to a zone with fresh air."

"I can smell it from here, in fact," said Miss Louise, wrinkling her nose. "And my sense of smell isn't what it used to be either, so that's saying something."

"I can't smell a thing if it's more than a foot away from my nose," said One-Eyed Willie. "Although, I've got to tell you, that's a huge relief given some of these humans and their love of dousing themselves with all sorts of odd fragrances. Why don't they just wear pleasant scents, like tuna or liver instead of strange chemical combinations?"

"I agree with you there," said Jinx. The door to the café opened, and a gust of wind ruffled his fur.

A barrel-chested man wearing a heavy black trench coat with greasy slicked-back dark hair walked in. He had a scruffy goatee, thick neck and the super-sized muscles of a professional bodybuilder or football player. He paused and glanced around the room as though looking for someone. Or could he be casing the place? Jinx's cat-tuition niggled. But, seeing as how he'd been blamed for things because of his appearance, he didn't want to judge and was a little ashamed of his suspiciousness.

The man suddenly noticed him. He took a few steps closer, bent down, and peered at him with beady dark eyes.

"Hey," he said to no one in particular. "Is that a baby monkey?"

Fine, forget about being Mr. Nice Guy. Jinx raised his hackles and flattened his ears.

"Baby monkey!" he cried in cat language, which in human came out as a hiss. "Get some glasses, buddy! Am I allowed to scratch him?"

Miss Louise twitched her whiskers. "I recommend taking the high road, dumpling," she advised. "Literally and figuratively. Come, sit by Maw-Maw." She patted the space beside her with her paw.

"Go for it!" said One-Eyed Willie. "If I had any claws left, I'd give the fella a swing with my mean left hook!"

"Don't do it!" called Miss Louise.

"I'll give you my next tuna crunchie to see you do it!" said Willie, batting his front paws in the air like he was fighting.

Jinx backed up, getting ready to pounce.

"Ha!" said Clarissa with a laugh from behind him. She scooped him up into her arms again and smoothed the fur down along his spine.

"This is Jinx, our newest adoptable cat," she said to the customer. "Would you like to pet him?"

"I really hope she's joking," muttered Jinx.

The man shook his head. "No, thanks," he said, smiling at Clarissa. His teeth had the brown stains of a frequent smoker and Jinx detected the unmistakable scent of cigar smoke on his breath and clothes. Pee-yew.

"At Paws-N-Pastries, we specialize in fostering homeless cats and promoting their adoptions," explained Clarissa.

"That's nice," said the man, again gazing around the café.

The bell over the front door jingled again, and a man in police uniform walked in.

"Hey Travis," called Cody, crossing to greet him. The two shook hands.

"Good to see you Cody," the officer replied. "I was just stopping in on my way to the station to buy tickets for the Black Cat Bash tomorrow night. My wife and kids can't wait."

"Awesome," said Cody. "I'm dropping off a couple of boxes of pumpkins now from Louis's family farm."

Jinx noticed the cigar-smoking customer paying attention as the men chatted, though he turned his back to them.

"What's this about a Black Cat Bash?" he asked Clarissa.

"We're hosting a Halloween costume party Saturday night," she explained, tucking a blonde curl behind her ear. "All of the proceeds will go towards the shelter and care of homeless animals."

"Ah, you don't say," said the man with a sly grin. "How much are tickets?"

"Ten dollars apiece," Clarissa informed.

"Great, I'll take one," said the man.

"Wonderful, thank you so much for your support!" said Clarissa. "Please follow me over to the register so I can ring up the sale and get you your ticket for tomorrow night's event."

"Perfect," said the man.

Clarissa put Jinx back down and led the man away.

Jinx backed up into a corner and watched from afar. The cigar-smoker reached into his pocket and took out a thick set of crisply folded bills. He licked his thumb and index finger and swiped two fives from the top, handing them to Clarissa.

She popped the cash into the drawer and tore an orange ticket from the roll on the counter. "Here you go," she said. "Don't forget to wear a costume."

"No problem," he said as he pocketed the ticket. "Oh, by the way, I passed the postal carrier on my way in. I offered to drop off the mail here to save him a trip. Here you go."

The guy reached into the inside pocket of his trench coat and took out a stack of newspaper advertisements and envelopes held together with a dirty rubber band. He placed them on the counter's shiny surface.

"Can you make sure the owner here gets this stuff?"

"Of course, thank you," said Clarissa, taking the mail and putting it on a shelf behind the bar.

"Have a nice day," the man said, winking at her. He then turned and left the café, keeping his head down as he walked past the police officers.

Hm, Jinx thought, feeling relieved once he was gone.

***

"Are people always this crazy when they're getting ready for a party?" asked Jinx. He, Miss Louise, and One-Eyed Willie were gathered on the perches of the climbing wall, watching Darcy, Velma, and Clarissa run about the cafe putting up final decorations. Harriet, the cook, hustled back and forth from the kitchen as fast she could, which was impressive considering her girth was almost equal to her height. She placed another tray of cupcakes on the buffet and stopped to catch her breath. Her short red curls were plastered to her brow that was damp with sweat.

Even Fletcher, who followed her carrying a plastic pumpkin filled with gourmet wrapped candies, looked nervous.

"Yes," answered Miss Louise and Willie at once.

A knock on the café's front door startled everyone and the cats and humans jumped. Jinx turned to view the entrance. Who could it be? Velma closed the café two hours ago and Clarissa had hung a sign stating they were closing early for the Black Cat Bash and those without tickets could purchase them at the door with a valid credit or debit card.

"I'll see who it is," Clarissa offered. She clicked on the flickering lights of one of the battery-operated candles she'd been placing around the room and set it back down before going to the door. The glow from the candles lent a spooky aura to the space and Jinx felt the fur on the back of his neck tingle.

Turning the bolt, Clarissa opened the door to a middle-aged, very anxious-appearing couple. The man held a cat carrier in his arms.

"I'm afraid we're closed right now," Clarissa said.

The woman wrung her hands, blinking back tears. "I'm so sorry to bother you, but we didn't know where else to go."

"Oh dear, what seems to be the trouble?" asked Clarissa.

The man glanced at his wife. "We'll figure this out, hon," he said to her before responding. "A few weeks ago, we discovered that a stray cat had given birth to a litter of kittens in our backyard. Thankfully, we were able to find good homes right away for the mom and most of the babies. These two are the only ones we haven't been able to place yet. They're twins, so we really want them to be adopted together."

"I agree," said Clarissa. "Why don't you take them to the county shelter next week? Or you can bring them back here if you prefer on Monday. We're quite busy now getting ready for an event."

"We know," said the man. "The problem is, we're moving out of town and we're leaving today. In an hour, in fact. The county shelter is already closed."

"Is there any way you could take these two?" The woman begged. "They're really the sweetest little girls."

Clarissa turned and caught Velma's eye. Jinx saw Velma nod. Clarissa smiled and turned back to the couple.

"All right," she said. "Come on in and let me grab the necessary paperwork."

***

"Hi!" said the twin all-white kittens in unison a half hour later. They sat next to each other on the plush cranberry-colored rug in the Kitty Corner and looked up with excited furry faces at Jinx and the others.

"I'm Twinkletoes!" said one.

"And I'm Sparklenose!" said the other.

"But you can call us Twinkle and Sparkle for short," said the first with a giggle.

"That's right, we're the Twinkies!" giggled Sparkle.

"You've got to be kidding," muttered Jinx, sliding his eyes to One-Eyed Willie.

"Well, aren't you two the cutest things!" exclaimed Miss Louise. She jumped down to the floor and rubbed noses with each of the twins— the equivalent of a double-cheek human kiss, as Jinx had learned.

"I declare, wouldn't you both look just precious with little pink diamond collars?" Miss Louise continued, gazing at the picture-perfect twins. "Come with me, dears, and let me show you around the hotel area. You can think of me and One-Eyed Willie up there"—she paused to point him out with her paw—"as the innkeepers. Jinx, the black cat, is a current resident at Paws-N-Pastries. We're not yet certain regarding the permanency of his stay."

The kittens nodded. "Sounds good," said Twinkle.

"We understand," said Sparkle.

"I was all-white like you girls once," said Willie. "Look what age has done to me," he chuckled and winked his one eye.

The twins gasped in horror.

"Oh, stop you old coot," Miss Louise said, shaking her head. "Don't worry girls, he's just kidding with you."

"Phew," they both said at once.

"Willie may not have been white, but he was a very handsome boy," said Miss Louise, giving him a special smile.

He smiled back. "Aw, shucks," he said.

Miss Louise was just demonstrating the use of the scratching post to the kittens when Velma appeared from the back carrying a cardboard box.

"It's time to get you all into your costumes!" she said eagerly, setting the box on the floor of the Kitty Corner.

Jinx frowned. "Is she talking to us?" he asked Willie.

"I hope not," replied Willie. "But I think she is."

Velma knelt, opened the box, and pulled out an assortment of Halloween pet attire.

Both he and Willie groaned at the same time.

A few minutes later, Miss Louise pranced out from behind the box, wearing a little crown and red cape.

"Woo-hoo!" she said. "Isn't my outfit amazing? I love it!"

"Of course you do," said Willie under his breath. "Very nice, dear," he called.

"I think I even have something that will fit our newest arrivals," said Velma, rustling in the box. "Yep, I do! Come here girls, let's get you both dressed for the party." She picked up the kittens and took them behind the box.

Sparkle and Twinkle emerged with glittery angel wings around their backs. They giggled as they looked at each other.

"You look fabulous!" They said in unison.

Jinx rolled his eyes.

"Now your turn." Uh-oh. He met Velma's gaze and gulped.

"Is this as bad as I think it is?" He asked Willie a minute later.

Willie laughed.

"I guess that's a yes," Jinx grumbled.

"I think you look cute," said Miss Louise.

"I didn't realize bats were cute," Jinx said grumpily, turning his head to look at the dark bat wings on either side of his back.

"Just go with it, son," said Willie.

"Let's see what you get," Jinx replied.

He and the other cats waited while Velma took Willie to the "backstage" dressing area.

"No, just no," they heard him say.

Jinx smiled.

"This is going to be good," said Miss Louise.

"Come on out!" shouted Sparkle, clapping her paws.

Slowly, Willie stepped out from behind the side of the box.

Jinx and the others erupted in laughter. This was the best thing he'd seen all day.

"Harrumph," said Willie. "This never happened." A pair of reindeer antlers sat on top of his head.

Chapter Five

Clarissa

The party was in full swing and Clarissa stood at the door taking tickets. She couldn't believe the turnout. Half of New Haven must be there tonight, and more were still arriving. Michael Jackson's "Thriller" played from the loudspeakers as costumed partygoers laughed and nibbled on the delectable treats laid out on the long buffet table against the far wall. Harriet had outdone herself, Clarissa thought, admiring the assortment of edible delights. Not only were there cupcakes and cookies featuring ghosts, pumpkins, and other Halloween scenes made out of icing and sugar work, but spookier goodies as well such as the popular "witches' fingers" and "eyeballs" crafted from rice crispies, almonds, raisins, and other everyday foods. An extra-large glass bowl in the center of the arrangement was filled with bright green punch and dry ice, sending swirling fog into the air like a bubbling cauldron.

The staff of Paws-N-Pastries had agreed to dress up like the characters from The Wizard of Oz. Velma wore a giant lion onesie, and thanks to the theater makeup she'd applied, appeared the spitting image of the Cowardly Lion. She stood talking with Professor Squiggly who had come dressed as Dumbledore from the Harry Potter franchise. Harriet passed a cookie to a child in a firefighter's outfit. She had chosen to be the Scarecrow, wearing a flannel shirt and overalls with hay sticking out from the neck and sleeves. Fletcher, meanwhile, was dressed all in silver as the Tin Man.

Clarissa smiled, watching him lean closer to Glinda the Good Witch. Of all of them, Darcy's costume was the most stunning transformation from her everyday self. She'd washed the black dye out of her hair, revealing it to be naturally cornsilk blonde. And she'd scrubbed the makeup off her face and removed her ear piercings. Clarissa would never have suspected that underneath the outer garb was a very pretty woman who appeared even younger than her actual age. Judging from the way Fletcher was looking at her, she bet he was thinking the same thing. Perhaps Darcy held the key to his heart after all.

"You look great, Dorothy," called a male voice approaching the café's entrance.

Turning, she saw Cody in his police uniform.

She gave him a playful punch on the arm. "I don't think your costume counts," she laughed as he passed her his ticket.

He chuckled. "I know," he said ruefully. "I've been working so much lately I didn't have time to pick up something else, but I wanted to stop by tonight and say hello."

"I'm glad," she replied.

He stepped inside as a mother with three children dressed as fairytale princesses walked up behind him.

"I'm so sorry," the woman said. "I just noticed the sign saying that you're accepting only credit or debit cards to pay for tickets at the door. I completely forgot to purchase tickets this week and all I brought with me is cash. I'd need change for a $50 though."

"Hm," said Clarissa. She didn't want to disappoint the children, all of whom had worried expressions on their faces. "We've locked the cash drawer for tonight, but I'm the manager here and I'll make this one exception."

"Oh, thank you so much!" said the woman, breathing a sigh of relief as her daughters clapped their hands and jumped up and down. "We heard that you have some adoptable cats, too, and we're interested in adding a pet to our family."

"I'll see you later at the buffet," whispered Cody.

"Sounds good," she said, nodding.

"Follow me," she told the woman, leading her and the girls inside. She made her way around the coffee bar to the cash register and unlocked it with her master key. The mother passed her the fifty-dollar bill as she pulled open the drawer to gather change.

However, the drawer was completely empty. Not a single coin lay inside. Clarissa was shocked. Where had the money gone? She searched in the crevices of the slots, hoping to find something, anything, but all she came up with a slip of blank paper. She shoved it hastily into her apron.

"Um, since you're interested in adoption, I'm going to waive the entrance fee for you tonight." She gave the woman a shaky smile and handed back the fifty.

"Thank you so much," the woman said, tucking it into her purse. "I really appreciate this. Let's go look at the kitties, girls." She steered her children towards the Kitty Corner as Clarissa hurried to locate Velma.

"I'm really sorry to interrupt," she said, cutting into Velma's conversation with

Professor Squiggly. "Could I speak to you privately for a minute?"

"Sure," Velma said. "I'll be right back, Alfred." She wiggled her fingers and Professor Squiggly smiled and popped a cookie into his mouth.

"What's wrong?" Velma asked, following Clarissa to an empty corner. "You look worried."

"Did you take the money out of the cash drawer?" Clarissa asked breathlessly.

Velma shook her head. "No, why?"

"It's gone."

"What do you mean, gone?" Velma asked.

"I mean, I just unlocked the register to get change for a lady who only had a fifty with her and is interested in adopting one of the cats for her daughters. And when I opened the drawer, it was completely empty."

Velma clutched her chest. "The only people who have master keys to the register are you and me."

"I know," Clarissa said miserably. "We've been robbed."

***

"Back-up will be here in a few minutes," Cody announced to the crowd, which had fallen silent. After she and Velma had informed him of the situation, he had taken charge immediately, directing Fletcher to the entrance and telling him not to let anyone leave while asking Darcy to turn off the music and Velma to flip on the bright overhead lights. Clarissa stood next him grimly at the front of the room while he called everyone's attention and announced that the café appeared to have been robbed during the party.

"We'll need to question everyone here," Cody continued. "We ask that you wait patiently until an officer has taken your statement."

People glanced at each other nervously, holding half-eaten treats in their hands, appetites now lost.

Cody withdrew a small notepad and pen from his pocket. "If anyone remembers something suspicious, please come find me immediately."

He motioned Clarissa and the other staff except for Fletcher aside. "I'm sorry this has happened, guys," he said. "But I promise I'll do my best to identify the culprit."

"Thank you," said Velma, tears streaming down her cheeks, leaving streaks of makeup.

Simone Laveau appeared from the crowd. She was dressed as Jasmine in a billowy blue top and pants that left her midriff bare.

"I think I saw something," she said coyly to Cody. "Perhaps I can share it with you privately, somewhere else?"

"Sorry, no can do," said Cody. "I need to stay here but am happy to hear what you have to say as long as we remain on the premises."

"Oh," said Simone with a look of disappointment. "I'm not sure it's that big of a deal, actually. I noticed several children putting candy in their pockets. I wasn't sure whether that was allowed."

"I see," said Cody. "I don't think that has any bearing to the case, but I appreciate your making sure."

"Of course," Simone murmured. "Let me give you my number in case you wish to ask me any other questions."

Clarissa tried not to roll her eyes as she recited her phone number.

After she turned away, Cody shook his head. "Whatever she's selling, I'm not buying," he said. "Not my type. By the way, the forensics team will need to wipe down the cash drawer for prints. I'd like to take a look at it myself."

"Okay," said Clarissa, leading him to the register. "The only thing I found inside was a blank piece of paper." She reached into the pocket of her apron and drew out the slip, handing it to Cody.

He turned it over and shrugged. "Unfortunately, there's nothing on it so I don't think it's a clue." He passed it back to her and she turned, tossing it into the trash can with a sigh. As she did so, her elbow bumped a nearby canister of cat treats, and one fell into the trash by accident.

Chapter Six

Jinx

"Did anyone but me see that tuna crunchie fall in the trash?" Jinx asked. However, no one answered. One-Eyed Willie had fallen asleep in his cat bed and Miss Louise appeared to be too busy giving herself a bath to respond. Twinkletoes and Sparklenose were purring and being passed back and forth between the three little girls and their mother who were all sitting on the floor in the Kitty Corner, cooing over them with delight.

"All righty then, I'm claiming dibs on the yummy," Jinx said. Rising, he jumped down from the chair where he'd been sitting and made his way through the waiting crowd to the coffee bar. Hopping up, he estimated the distance to the opening of the waste bin, did some kitty physics in his head regarding proper angle and force, and made a flying leap.

Thankfully, his calculations were correct, and he sailed directly into the opening and dropped inside without a sound. "I can't believe that worked," he said to himself as he began to paw the miscellaneous bits of refuse, searching for the dropped treat. Pee-yew. He wrinkled his nose. What was that smell? He couldn't even detect the scent of his favorite snack with the overpowering odor. Where was it coming from? He sifted through some napkins as he tracked down the stench, finally discovering the source beneath a half-eaten cookie. A slip of paper. The same one Clarissa had found in the cash drawer. He sniffed it and gagged. Yep, no doubt about it, that was the same one. But wait—hadn't Clarissa and Cody said it was blank? In the dim light filtering through the trash can, he noticed faint traces of handwriting left after someone tried to erase the words. When he read them, he knew what he had to do, stink and all. After all, what cat doesn't love justice?

Grabbing the paper in his mouth, he backed into a corner and began jumping around, trying to make as much noise as possible. He was perfectly aware that he could have hopped back out the way he'd come in, but no one else knew that. He just hoped the ploy would work.

Turned out that it worked even better than he anticipated. After a particularly forceful collision with the side of the can, it tipped, and fell over completely, landing against the floor with a crash. Trash spilled everywhere, and he scampered out with the paper in his mouth.

"Jinx!" cried Clarissa, running up to him with Cody at her heels.

Ordinarily, he would have made his cutest 'I'm sorry' face and played on the humans' sympathy in hopes of cuddles and snacks, but this time was different. So instead, he hissed and made a beeline for the storage area, glancing back to ensure Clarissa and Cody were following. They were. He ran into the kitchen and darted through Harriet's legs as she was washing dishes.

"Eep!" she cried.

"Sorry, Harriet!" said Clarissa as she and Cody jogged past.

Jinx knew there had to be one around here somewhere. He ran in a wide arc until he found what he was looking for—the janitor's closet. The door was slightly ajar, and he raced inside, stopped, and waited. He dropped the piece of paper on the floor and laid down beside it.

Feet pounded on the tile outside. The door opened, and Cody stepped inside. He reached for the string attached to the single overhead bulb and pulled. A dim yellow light shone into the small space.

"Oh Jinx, you silly kitty," said Clarissa, coming into the closet behind Cody. She knelt beside Jinx. "Hey, what do you have there?" She picked up the slip of paper he'd dropped onto the floor.

"Cody, this is the piece of paper I found in the cash drawer," she said, standing back up. "I think there's something written on it after all, see?" She held it up to the light.

They both peered at it closely. "*The money's due—with interest. Saturday night. No police—or else,*" read Cody. Clarissa gasped.

"Did you find Jinx?" called Velma, suddenly appearing in the doorway.

"He's right here," replied Clarissa, scooping him up into her arms.

"You're just the person I wanted to talk to," said Cody as the trio stepped out of the closet back into the large bright kitchen.

"Do you know anything about this note?" he asked Velma, showing it to her. "Someone used an eraser to try and scrub what was written on it, but the marks are still visible when viewed in the correct light." He read the contents aloud.

"Yes," wailed Velma, bursting into tears. "All right, I confess. I've wanted to open Paws-N-Pastries for years but couldn't find a bank that would give me a loan. So, I decided to take an alternate route to get the money for the initial investment."

"In other words, you used a loan shark," said Clarissa.

Velma nodded. "Yes. At the time I figured the ends justified the means, but it didn't turn out that way at all."

"I'll bet," said Cody, crossing his arms over his chest.

"I couldn't make the repayments on the loan on time," she continued. "I began receiving threatening notes. I didn't know what to do. So, I proposed the Black Cat Bash to raise enough money," she said miserably. "I was hoping to make enough of a profit to donate at least a little to the animals."

"Oh, Velma." Clarissa said sadly, shaking her head.

"What's this about Saturday night?" asked Cody. "And what did you do with the money from the register?"

"The money's right here," said Velma, bending down and removing her giant lion paw slipper. She reached inside and pulled out a large stack of dollar bills. "I was supposed to give it to the loan shark's business associate tonight. The problem is, I don't know who it is or how to find them."

Realization dawned on Jinx all at once. He leapt out of Clarissa's arms.

"Where's he off to now?" Cody asked. "The little guy looks like he's on a mission."

Jinx ran back into the main area of the café and lifted his nose. Yep, he knew it. The person who had written the note was here. He wound his way through the crowd until he found someone dressed as the Phantom of the Opera, wearing the signature long black cape and white mask. Crouching back on his haunches, he prepared to make the high jump, hoping he was strong enough. With a hiss, he leaped onto the Phantom's shoulder and batted at the mask.

"Hey?!" yelled the man as his disguise fell to the ground. His breath reeked of the unmistakable scent of cigar smoke, which had been strong enough to leave its mark on everything the man touched.

"That's the same guy who delivered the mail for the postal carrier a couple of days ago," said Clarissa.

"And that's where I found this note—it was tucked into the stack," cried Velma.

"You're under arrest, buddy," said Cody, grabbing the guy's beefy arms and pinning them behind his back. At that moment, the front door burst open and five uniformed officers strode into the room.

"I want my lawyer," the henchman seethed.

Epilogue

Jinx

Jinx munched on his bowl of kibble as Cody and Clarissa sat on the sofa together, sipping mugs of hot chocolate. The café was quiet since it was after hours and they were only ones there besides the cats.

"Wow, what a week," said Clarissa. "It's been such a whirlwind."

"That it has," agreed Cody.

"I'm really glad the judge let Velma off with probation and community service," she said. "She meant well but was unfortunately misguided."

"Agreed," said Cody. "This was her first offense, and it was pretty obvious that she simply let her desire to help homeless animals cloud her better judgment. I think this will be a good lesson for her."

"I do, too," said Clarissa.

"She did make one very wise decision, though," Cody grinned.

"Oh? What's that?" Clarissa asked.

"Hiring you," he said.

Jinx saw Clarissa's cheeks turn pink. "Thank you," she said. "I'm glad to be here, and I intend to do my best to help Velma turn things around."

"I know if anyone can do it, it's you," said Cody.

"Another good thing came from the Black Cat Bash," said Clarissa. "Remember the twin kittens? Sparklenose and Twinkletoes were both adopted by the woman wanting change who came in with her three daughters that night."

"That's great," said Cody. "I'm happy that some silver linings that have come out of all this. I learned earlier today that Giuseppe Giancolo—our Phantom of the Opera who had been intimidating Velma—ratted out the guy he was working for, who is a pretty well-known character on the criminal circuit. We got enough to shut down his whole con operation and send him away for a long time."

"That's wonderful," said Clarissa. "What a relief!"

"I have two questions for you," Cody said, draining the last of his hot chocolate and setting the mug on the coffee table.

"What are they?' asked Clarissa curiously.

"First, would you like to have dinner with me next Saturday night?"

Clarissa grinned. "I'd love to."

A few beats of silence passed as they gazed into each other's eyes.

Finishing his dinner, Jinx felt drowsy. He curled into his cat bed as his eyelids began to droop.

"What's the second question?" He heard Clarissa say.

"What's going to happen to Jinx?" asked Cody. "Have you found anyone who wants to adopt him?"

Jinx's ears perked up.

"As a matter of fact, I have," Clarissa responded. "Me."

Jinx lifted his head.

"My apartment felt a little lonely," she continued. "And I decided I could really use a roommate. Who better than Jinx?"

"I'd say he's proven to be good luck," Cody said. "We would never have caught up with the bad guys without his help."

"Exactly," said Clarissa. "He's not a cursed cat at all. Sometimes it's just a matter of finding your place in the world."

"There's no place like home, after all," Cody said with a smile.

Indeed, thought Jinx happily. *Sometimes dreams really do come true.* And with that, he settled down to sleep.

For more Holiday Pet Sleuth Mysteries go to: https://amzn.to/3Ryn2Ma

Sneak Peek:
The Witch with a Glitch

*If you enjoyed **Halloween Hi-Jinx**, you may also enjoy **The Witch with a Glitch**, a YA coming-of-age short story by Annee Jones featuring a very special heroine and her lovable kitty companion.*

Chapter One

"Voila!" Esme Green said, smiling at her Potions table partner, Paisley Renfrew. She poured a little of the brew she'd been hard at work concocting for the past hour from its bubbling beaker into a small test tube and handed it to her friend. Paisley frowned as she lifted the vial to her nostrils and gave it a sniff. Her pert freckle-covered nose wrinkled.

"Um, are you sure you followed the directions correctly, Esme? The spell book says the Growing Potion ought to be the color of spinach, but this kind of looks more like split-pea soup – and smells like it too." Paisley eyed the potion uncertainly.

"I'm pretty sure I did," Esme replied, swiveling back to her grimoire, which was laid open on the desk. She flipped through pages 324-328 containing the instructions for today's assignment. She thought she'd done everything right. Hadn't she? Running her index finger over the swirly script, she tried again to make sense of the letters, but as usual, they kept jumping off the page and mixing themselves up, so that she couldn't make hide nor hair of their proper order. She blinked, wishing they would just stay in place for once. Did everyone have this much trouble reading their spell books? She glanced around. It certainly didn't seem like it. Nearby, other witches were confidently stirring pots of perfect spinach-colored liquid and putting their calculations to the test by having their partners drink the potion in front of Professor Buble, who watched with his grade book open and pointy pencil in hand. If successful, the Growing Potion would make the subject grow three feet taller. Esme watched as the most popular witch in school and her competition for Class President, Hesper Frost, proudly showed off her brew. Hesper flipped a lock of her white-blond hair over one shoulder and smiled as her table partner, Rudy Templeton, downed the contents of his glass in one gulp. Rudy was already three feet taller – as well as three feet wider - than everyone else in the class, but sure enough he promptly sprouted another three feet before everyone's eyes. Just as everyone thought the potion had finished taking effect, Rudy grew another foot.

"Awesome, dude," he said, looking down at himself.

"Excellent job, Miss Frost, not only did you earn a perfect score, but you went over and above, quite literally," said Professor Buble with a chuckle. "I'll give you extra credit for this assignment – not that you need it, of course."

Hesper smiled, her frosty pink lips sparkling.

Esme turned back to her potion. She exchanged a worried glance with Paisley.

Professor Buble continued to walk around the room with his grade book and pencil, marking off those who had completed the assignment correctly, which was quite obvious to see. His bald head gleamed under the harsh fluorescent lighting.

"I really don't know about this," said Paisley nervously.

"Ah, Esmeralda Green," said Professor Buble, coming to their table. "How is your potion coming along?"

"Very well, sir," Esme replied. "At least, I think," she added.

"Let's have a look-see then, shall we?" The professor removed a monocle from a pocket of his black cape and clasped it over his right eye. He peered at the glass vial in Paisley's hand.

"Hm," he said. "I'm sorry Esme, but I'll have to take points off for color. No one likes split-pea soup," he said with a shudder. "Go on, Miss Renfrew, drink up, let's give the thing a go and see if it does what it's supposed to at least," he directed.

Paisley pinched her nostrils closed with the thumb and index finger of her right hand and brought the fizzing vial to her mouth with her left, hesitating just before it touched her lips.

"On the count of three, then," said Professor Buble with a nod. "One...two...three."

Esme's eyes widened as she watched her friend swallow the liquid. She crossed her fingers. Please let this work.

"Ew," said Paisley, grimacing.

"How do you feel?" asked the teacher.

Paisley's reply came in the form of a loud belch. Immediately, her right arm began growing while the left was shrinking, and her left leg began growing while the right was shrinking. Caught off balance with her suddenly mismatched limbs, she toppled over onto the stone floor with a yelp.

"Oh dear," said Professor Buble, clucking his tongue. He scribbled something into his notebook. "Miss Green, I'm afraid this is the fourth assignment in a row you've been unable to pass."

"I tried my best," said Esme, tears pricking the backs of her eyes. The teacher tucked his pencil behind one of his ears and reached into his cape again, this time drawing out his wand.

"For what it's worth, I believe you," he said before waving the wand over poor Paisley who was floundering about on the floor like a fish out of water.

Silver sparks shot out of the wand and in a flash Paisley's limbs had corrected themselves to their normal length. She got up and dusted off her cape. "Phew," she said. "That was an experience."

"I'm so sorry," said Esme. "I hope you're not mad at me."

Paisley shook her head, her red curls bouncing. "I'm not," she said. "We've been best friends since our first year at Salem Academy, and I know you didn't do it on purpose."

"Thank you," Esme replied with a faint smile.

"And you've still got my vote for Class President," Paisley added. "Frankly, I'd rather a toad be Class President over Hesper." She made a face in Hesper's direction.

"I'm not sure whether that's supposed to be a compliment, but I'll take it," said Esme.

"Miss Green, I think I may have an idea of what is going on here," the professor said, interrupting the girls. He set his grade book down and crossed his arms over his chest thoughtfully.

"Oh?" Esme asked, hopeful. "Do you think there was some sort of problem with one of the ingredients I used? Perhaps one of them was expired?"

Professor Buble shook his head. "There was nothing wrong with the ingredients. I'm referring you to Dr. Violet Twombly for a full mental evaluation. I suspect we're dealing with a case of dys-HEX-ia."

***

The sound of light clapping woke her up. Esme sat up on the purple velvet chaise in the doctor's office. Dr. Twombly was seated in a chair nearby, her lilac-hued hair pulled back into a tight bun.

"Did you have a nice nap, dear?" the doctor asked.

Esme yawned. "I don't remember a thing," she said.

"That was the point," said Dr. Twombly. "It's easier for me to delve inside people's brains telepathically when they're sound asleep. There's much less interference that way."

"So do I have dyx-HEX-ia?" Esme asked, twisting her fingers with trepidation.

"Yes," Dr. Twombly. "According to the Diagnostic Statistical Manual version 1,007, used for diagnosing glitches that affect witches, you meet the criteria."

"Oh no!" Esme cried. "Is there a cure?"

To her surprise, the doctor laughed. "Child, there's no need to fret." She waved her hand in the air. "Personally, I don't really believe in this whole diagnosing thing. It seems every year the council adds fifty or so more maladies to the textbook and removes fifty others. In other words, it's all a bunch of hooey. The bottom line is that all witches will face some sort of glitch or two in their lifetime. No witch is perfect."

"Except Hesper Frost," Esme muttered, staring down at the black toes of her Doc Marten boots peeking out from the under the bottom of her cape.

"I heard that," Dr. Twombly said. "Just remember there may be more to someone that meets the eye."

"Hm." Esme wasn't convinced. Hesper Frost had recently joined the academy and with her stunning looks and stellar grades, quickly catapulted to the status of most popular girl in school as well as the teachers' pet. Neither Hesper nor the other girls in her clique paid any mind to anyone they felt wasn't up to their standards – and that included Esme. Personally, she wouldn't want to be one of Hesper's fawning groupies anyway.

"What happens now?" she asked the doctor.

"You'll be given accommodations," Dr. Twombly replied with a kind smile. "In fact, I've already arranged for them." She rose and walked toward the closed door of her office.

"Accommodations?" repeated Esme. "Like what?"

Dr. Twombly opened the door with a flourish. In walked a fat black cat with green eyes.

"Like me," said the cat.

Esme's mouth dropped open. "I get a cat?"

"Esme, meet Rafael. Rafael will be your recorder," said Dr. Twombly.

"What's a recorder?" asked Esme, eyeing the cat as it leaped up into a chair and began smoothing its whiskers with a paw.

"Rafael will accompany you to your classes and memorize the lectures to recite back to you as needed," the physician explained.

"You can really do that?" Esme asked Rafael, surprised.

"Yep," he said. "People seriously don't give cats enough credit."

"He will also be your study partner," Dr. Twombly continued.

"In other words, you're stuck with me now, kid," Rafael said.

Esme wasn't sure that was necessarily a good thing. However, Dr. Twombly seemed very certain he'd be able to help her, so she may as well as give the cat a try.

"All right," she agreed meekly. "After all, what do I have to lose?"

Available Now

THE WITCH WITH A GLITCH

Available here:

https://books2read.com/The-Witch-With-A-Glitch

Esmeralda "Esme" Green is trying her best to earn her marks at Salem Academy, but she keeps mixing up the directions in her spell book and can't manage to spell "abracadabra" correctly no matter how hard she tries.

After one too many spells gone wrong, her professor finally suggests she be evaluated for dys-HEX-ia. This can't come at a worse time since Esme is running for Class President against the most popular witch in school, Hesper Frost.

Unfortunately, Esme's diagnosis gets into the wrong hands and soon she's accused of not even being a "real" witch.

Can Esme and her trusted cat familiar, Rafael, prove to Hesper and the rest of the class that there's nothing wrong with being a witch with a glitch?

LOVE AND PUMPKIN SPICE LATTES–

A Pumpkin Patch Romance

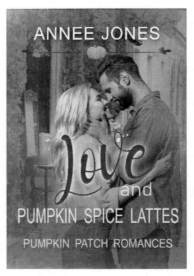

Available here:

https://books2read.com/Love-and-Pumpkin-Spice-Lattes

A surprise visit from an old friend is th beginning of something sweet for a barista... but not everyone is in love with the idea. Who would want to sabotage this budding romance?

Piper loves her life. She runs a small coffee shop that's quickly become a favorite in town. She has great customers, wonderful coworkers, and not a complaint in the world. When her coworker notices that one of her customers is paying extra attention to her, she finds it endearing. Trey is sweet, kind, and funny, but she doesn't like him like that. She's happy with things the way they are.

When Gus, an old friend from school, returns to town and stops by to pay her a visit, she couldn't be more thrilled. He's the same great guy he's always been and just as handsome. Their relationship falls right back in place. It's as if he never left. Before long, they plan a trip to the pumpkin patch for old time's sake, but the nostalgia is short-lived when someone makes ominous threats and even follows them on one of their adventures.

Something is brewing, and it's not just a budding romance. When Gus and Piper uncover the truth, will it pull them closer or send them running in opposite directions?

Love and Pumpkin Spice Lattes is a sweet contemporary romance that will warm your heart.

<u>One-Click</u> *Love and Pumpkins Spice Latte* <u>today!</u>

Coming Soon
BELLE – Runaway Brides of the West

October 2022

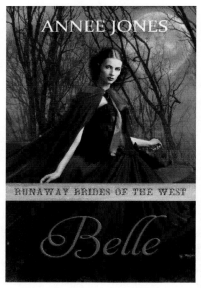

Available here:

https://books2read.com/Belle-Runaway-Brides

Threatened with blackmail, will Belle give in to the theatre director's demands and become his bride? Or will she choose to trust a man with a penchant for

disappearing with the secrets of her past?

When the director of a traveling theatre troupe asks ballerina Belle Hathaway to become not only his star on the stage but also beyond it as his bride, how can she refuse? Especially given the details of her past that she will do anything to keep hidden.

However, when she begins falling for the troupe's handsome yet mysterious magician, Belle's secrets begin to quickly catch up with her and her very life could be at stake. Suddenly, she must decide whether to marry the ruthless director or trust a man she's afraid could disappear just when she needs him most.

JUSTICE FOR GINGER–

Thanksgiving Brides

November 2022

Available here:

https://books2read.com/Justice-for-Ginger

Mrs. Charlotte Dunbar has been widowed for longer than she was a wife, but that doesn't mean she doesn't like a good engagement or the drama of two young people coming together! Especially when she feels they just need

a little help to see the match was meant to be.

Five years ago, Ginger Carlyle turned down a marriage proposal that everyone, including Jacob Noble, thought she would agree to.

Five years ago, Jacob Noble took a job in a northern California mining town that he hoped would help him to forget the love he'd left behind in Ashton. But there was no way he could forget Ginger, or his own broken heart.

Back in Ashton, Ginger has been beset by tragedy after tragedy. After her father's death, she is the only one who can care for her ailing mother and manage the family house and land. Selling eggs and baked goods to make ends meet, Ginger and her mother survive out of sheer determination and hard work. But hard work isn't enough when the bank comes looking for the mortgage payments. Unable to tell her mother the truth about their dire financial circumstances, Ginger will have to work even harder to make sure that their Thanksgiving holiday is as joyful as it always was when her father was alive.

However, after Ginger is accused of stealing from her new employer, her whole world is turned upside down. She's dragged to the sheriff's office where she's shocked to discover the new deputy is none other than the very man whose proposal she turned down all those years ago. Can she trust Jacob to help prove her innocence? Or is he still harboring a grudge against her for refusing his hand in marriage?

As the past is re-visited and secrets come to light, is there hope that justice will be Ginger's in time for Thanksgiving?

Trust the local matchmaker to make sure!

STARLIGHT INN–Christmas at the Inn

November 2022

Available here:

https://books2read.com/Starlight-Inn

Caught in a snowstorm on Christmas Eve, Hope has no choice but spend the holiday at the Starlight Inn. Will she be touched by the magic of Christmas with a little help from a handsome stranger?

Hope Garland is at a crossroads. Nothing she does feels like it's getting her to where she wants to be in life... It's time for a change. Leaving everything in Dallas behind was a difficult choice, but she'll have to make sacrifices to get the life she's always wanted, even if that means being away from home for Christmas so she'll be able to make her first shift on time.

Determined to reach her destination, Hope doesn't stop even when a snowstorm threatens. But after a near miss on the highway, she finally decides to pull over and have a coffee before she keeps going. But the snow isn't showing any sign of stopping and Hope will have to spend the night at a nearby inn.

The Starlight Inn is the perfect place to spend Christmas Eve, and Hope is swept away in the comfort and cheer of the holiday—but can she put aside her worry over her new job and take the time to really appreciate what Christmas has to offer?

Like it or not, Hope is snowed in at the Starlight Inn. Could handsome stranger Nicholas White, also stranded by the snowstorm, help her put things into perspective? Can she set things right before it's too late?

CHRISTMAS CAT-astrophe–
Holiday Pet Sleuth Mysteries
November 2022

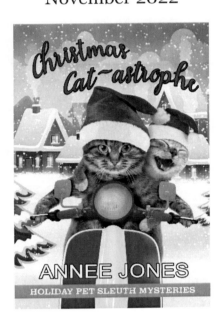

Available here:
https://books2read.com/Christmas-CAT-astrophe

It's beginning to look a lot like arson this Christmas season…

The Cat Café is buzzing with excitement this holiday season as they prepare for the Holiday Fur Ball & Silent Auction. As Tinsley and her crew put the finishing touches on the treats and decorations, she can't help but daydream about the new animal shelter she hopes to build with the money from the auction.

The excitement soon fizzles, however, when a fire breaks out at the café with the fur babies inside. Thankfully, they're rescued by firefighters and all safe and sound. But everyone at the Cat Café is shocked when the fire's cause is determined to be arson. With the future of the new shelter now on shaky ground, Tinsley knows she must find the culprit before they try again.

Even if she has to work with the handsome but know-it-all representative from the ball's big tech sponsor, Nick Greenly.

Perhaps rescue cat Jingle and his feline friends may have some ideas that could help solve the case? But time is running out...can they pinch the Grinch before he or she ruins the Holiday Fur Ball and spoils everyone's Christmas too?

Find out the fate of the beloved Cat Café and the new shelter and brighten your holidays by reading Christmas CAT-astrophe today!

KATRINA – Christmas Quilt Brides

December 2022

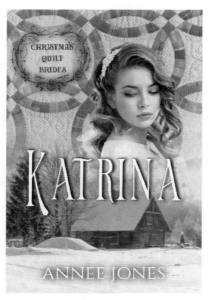

Available here:

https://books2read.com/Katrina-Christmas-Quilts

She knew the trip could be difficult, but she never imagined it'd change her life...

An unfortunate stagecoach accident leaves Katrina with no memory of who she is and where she was headed. The only clues to her identity are stitched in hand-sewn quilt, but to unravel them she must traverse across the countryside and find someone willing to answer her many questions.

Luke, the man who saved her after the accident and is now providing shelter for her, volunteers to travel with her. Their journey and those they meet along the way provide some clues, but unless she can stitch the pieces together, she may never learn the truth about who she is and why she was traveling on that fateful day.

Will she and Luke find the answers she so desperately needs or have memories faded and secrets remained intact?

FROSTY CAKE BY FLANNERY–
Old Timey Holiday Kitchen
December 2022

Available here:

https://books2read.com/Flannery

Does Flannery stand a chance of winning this year's holiday baking contest and the heart of the man she loves, when her main competition for both is her most bitter rival?

Flannery White is convinced that the way to a man's heart is through his stomach. And if she has her way, she'll be engaged to Divine, Colorado's most eligible bachelor, Warren Kane, by the time Christmas Day arrives.

The plan is simple. She'll enter the town's Christmas baking competition, impress him with her recreation of his favorite dessert, and find herself suddenly engaged to the steadfastly unaware object of her affections.

The only problem? Flannery is a disaster in the kitchen. And to make matters worse, her rival, Stella, is on the hunt for her own happily ever after with Warren, no matter the cost.

Thankfully, Flannery's best friend in the whole world, Sam Jolly, is ready to help her. As the son of a grocer, Sam knows his ingredients and his way around the kitchen. However, Sam's been keeping a little secret - he's been head-over-heels in love with Flannery since they were children.

Will Sam be able to put aside his love for Flannery to see her happily engaged to another man? Or will Flannery discover that true love might wear a flour-covered apron instead of an expensive suit?

A Note From Annee

Thank you so much for reading my book—I hope you enjoyed it. If so, please consider taking a moment to leave a review. Not only do good reviews help increase visibility of books you consider worthwhile, but they also let hard-working authors know that their stories make a difference. If my books put a smile on your face, touch your heart, or make you think—well, that's worth everything to me!

Sincerely yours,

Annee

Amazon ~ **Goodreads** ~ **Bookbub**

About the Author

Author Annee Jones writes heartwarming romance, fantasy, cozy mystery, and more. She is passionate about writing stories that offer readers a place where dreams come true! Professionally, Annee works as a disability counselor where she helps her clients navigate through complex medical and legal systems while rediscovering their wholeness in Spirit.

Annee enjoys practicing Barre and yoga in her free time, as well as spending time with her daughter and, of course, reading.

Subscribe to Annee's Newsletter on her **Website**

Find Annee's books on **Amazon** ~ **Goodreads** ~ **Bookbub**

Join Annee's private Facebook reader group, **Annee's Angels**

Connect with Annee on her **FB Author Page**

Made in United States
North Haven, CT
04 October 2023

42341717R00054